THE EXCHANGE STUDENT

AN EROTIC ADVENTURE

VICTORIA RUSH

VOLUME 28

JADE'S EROTIC ADVENTURES - BOOK 28

COPYRIGHT

The Exchange Student © 2020 Victoria Rush

Cover Design © 2020 PhotoMaras

FEEL THE RUSH:

Jade's Erotic Adventures – Book 1

When lonely divorcée Jade seeks to broaden her horizons, she's invited to a private dinner event which promises to stimulate all of her senses. Wearing nothing but masquerade masks, dinner guests receive special service under the table while their fellow diners look on...

The Dinner Party

Jade's Erotic Adventures - Book 2

Jade discovers an exotic adventure club where strangers meet to explore each other's bodies in mysterious dark rooms. Using special effects to project swirling light patterns onto their figures, the shifting shadows provide just enough illumination to highlight their naked bodies while protecting their identities...

The Dark Room

Jade's Erotic Adventures - Book 3

Jade discovers a yoga club where members stretch and explore each other's bodies in the buff. She books an appointment, and during the first session meets a young redhead who tantalizes her with her flexibility and stunning body...

Naked Yoga

For the uninhibited...

I received a text back from Luna when she got home from school saying pizza sounded great, but by then I'd finished most of my shopping, so I headed back a bit earlier than planned. When I pulled into the driveway, I didn't open the garage door like usual because I wanted to sneak my new fabric design in without her seeing it. Opening the door softly, I tiptoed down the hall and up the stairs, hoping to hide the material in my closet.

But as I approached my bedroom, I heard a soft buzzing sound and I paused at the partially closed door, peering through the crack. Luna was lying buck naked on my bed with a vibrator humming loudly between her legs. I recognized it immediately as my Rabbit vibrator and she was holding the end of it with two hands while she pressed the flapping ears tightly against her pussy.

Instantly aroused in a fit of passion, I placed the fabric bag down on the floor and unzipped my pants, thrusting my fingers under my soaking panties. As I watched Luna ramming the dildo in and out of her bare cunny, I trilled my clit rapidly, feeling my knees beginning to weaken. She looked even more beautiful with a soft flush filling her face and her pointy tits jiggling on her chest as she rolled her hips and flexed her arms, fucking herself with the buzzing vibrator.

As she began to arch her back and widen her mouth in mounting ecstasy, it took every ounce of my willpower not to barge through the door and take her into my arms. The more she tensed her body and arched her back, the closer my own orgasm steamrolled toward me. When she suddenly grunted and began jerking her body forward and back in the midst of a powerful orgasm, I felt my juices spraying all over my hand and jeans resting halfway down my thighs...

1

———————

I almost missed the ad while rushing out of the grocery store after a long day of work. Tucked away in a corner of the bulletin board near the exit door was a small poster with the headline *Earn Extra Income Hosting a Foreign Exchange Student.* I paused for a moment, then pulled my cart closer to the board to read the message:

Earn money while helping a foreign student expand their cultural horizons. There's no better way to learn a new language and appreciate other cultures than to live with someone from another part of the world. By hosting a young person from a different country, you promote friendship, understanding, and cooperation in your home and community. Welcome a foreign exchange student into your home today and open the door to an exciting new world of experiences. Contact exchangehost.com for more info.

After reading the ad, I suddenly became aware of how hard my heart was pounding in my chest. I'd lived alone after separating from my husband more than two years ago, and my big house had become far too quiet and lonely. Having never had children of my own, the idea of hosting a young person from another country seemed a perfect fit. I'd have someone to liven up my daily routine while helping the student develop a sense of independence in an exciting new environment.

When I got home, I went to the agency's website and read everything I could about the program. The more I learned, the more excited I became. I wasn't interested in the small monthly stipend I'd earn hosting the student so much as the sense of adventure taking in a boarder from a different country. It would be an opportunity to share cultural experiences, improve my foreign language skills, and make new friendships.

The following morning, I called first thing to book an appointment for an interview. When I got to their office, the receptionist escorted me into the director's suite where a smartly dressed woman in her fifties invited me to make myself comfortable while she took a seat in the opposite armchair.

"Welcome, Ms. Robertson," she said. "My name is Elise Laurent, the director of Exchange Host student exchange services. What brings you to our office today?"

"I'm interested in hosting a foreign exchange student," I said.

"I see you're here by yourself. Do you live alone?"

"Yes," I said, crossing my legs defensively. "Do you accept applications from single women?"

"Of course," she said. "It all depends on the individual's circumstances and motivation. Our primary concern is finding a safe and supportive environment for our clients. May I ask what attracts you to our program?"

"I saw an ad for your services at the supermarket. I've

never had any children, and I like the idea of helping a young person supplement their education in a different country. With so much conflict and misunderstanding between countries and cultures, this seems an ideal way to foster better communication and friendship."

"You seem primarily focused on the benefits to the *student*," the director nodded. "What advantages do you see for you, personally?"

"It's not about the money, if that's what you mean. I'd do it for free, if that were an option. I live alone and work from home, so I have limited opportunity for social interaction. To be honest, I think it would be fun to have someone else to share my house with. Especially a young person who I could foster and take under my wing. I could take her shopping, go out to restaurants, visit national parks–it could be fun for both of us."

"So you're looking to host a female student only?"

"Not necessarily. I'd consider either gender, but I think it would be more fun hosting a girl."

The director nodded, scribbling some notes on a notepad.

"You say money isn't a consideration. May I ask what you do for a living?"

"I'm a freelance graphic artist. I help develop ads, logos, websites, and media campaigns for corporate clients."

"Do you own your home?"

"I guess technically the bank owns it until the mortgage is paid off," I chuckled. "But yes, I'm the sole title owner."

"Umm," the director hummed, scribbling some more notes. "Do you have an extra room and bath available for another occupant?"

"Yes," I said. "Frankly, that's another reason I'm considering this. My house is far too large for one person. I'll feel better making better use of the extra space and helping the environment by wasting less."

"Um-hmm," the Ms. Laurent nodded. "And you feel you'll have enough free time away from your work and other responsibilities to give your charge proper attention and care? It's not like taking in a boarder–these students will need oversight and companionship. They'll be a long way from home in a whole new environment. It's more akin to a foster parent situation."

"Absolutely," I said. "Being self-employed means I can make my own hours and work around my guest's schedule. I'm looking forward to taking her under my wing and making a new friend. Like I said, I'm not doing it for the money."

"Okay," the woman said, putting down her notepad. "We'll need you to fill in an application and provide three references. Then I'll need your approval to run a criminal record check and credit check. If everything pans out, we'll begin contacting you with possible candidates to find a good fit. The whole process can take two or three months and with a new school year approaching, you'll need to get started soon."

"Sounds good," I said, rising from my chair and extending my hand. "Thank you for your time and assistance, Ms. Laurent. I'll look forward to hearing back from you at your earliest opportunity. Let me know if you need any more information in the meantime."

"It's been my pleasure," she said. "Thank you for your interest in our program. I think you'll find this experience enriching and rewarding on both sides. My assistant will help you with the paperwork. We'll be in touch soon."

After filling in the application, I drove home with a sense of excitement wondering who the agency would find to connect me with. I had no idea what age, sex, or nationality the student would be and that was part of the attraction. It would be a whole new experience for both of us. But after a few weeks of not hearing from the agency, I began to wonder if they were having second thoughts about my candidacy. I'd checked with my references who told me they'd already been contacted, and I knew there wouldn't be any issues with my background or credit check, so with only a few weeks left before the start of the new school year, I placed a call to the director.

"Exchange Host," the receptionist said, answering the phone.

"May I speak with Ms. Laurent?" I said.

"May I ask who's calling?"

"My name is Jade Robertson. I had an interview with Ms. Laurent a couple of months ago and haven't heard back. I was just hoping for an update."

"One moment please," the receptionist said.

"Hello, Ms. Robertson," the director said when she picked up her extension.

"I'm sorry to bother you," I said. "But I haven't heard back from you and I know we're getting close to the start of another academic year. I was wondering if you had any problems with my application or if you'd vetted any potential candidates."

"No," the director said. "Your application came through with flying colors. Unfortunately, it was processed a bit late and all of the hosting spots for the new school year have been filled."

"That's disappointing to hear," I said. "So I guess I'll have to wait another year for consideration?"

"Not necessarily," she said. "We have a number of students who seek to transfer mid-year. There may be another opportunity as we approach the end of the first semester. We'll contact you if anything becomes available."

"Okay, thank you, Ms. Laurent."

I hung up, feeling dejected about prematurely getting my hopes up. The closer we'd gotten to the start of the school year, the more excited I'd become about having a new housemate. Now I'd have to wait a whole other year to have the opportunity to host a student.

For a while, I considered putting an ad in the local university newspaper offering a room for board, but I knew it wouldn't be the same. There was something about taking in a young international student that added an extra allure for me. I'd have the chance to nurture someone who really depended on me while we explored each other's language and culture. In the end, I decided to hold off, hoping to try again next year.

But much to my surprise, I received a message from Ms. Laurent a couple of months later indicating that she had a new candidate lined up for the spring semester. I picked up the phone and called her immediately.

"Hello, Ms. Laurent," I said excitedly when she picked up the phone. "It's Jade Robertson. I got your message regarding a possible candidate for the spring semester, and I'm still interested."

"That's wonderful news," she said. "We're ready to finalize the placement if you're sure you're ready to proceed."

"Absolutely," I said, still catching my breath.

"Would you like to view the student's profile before

making a final commitment? We can send it to you via email if you prefer."

I paused for a moment, hearing my heart pounding in my chest. As eager as I was for more details, I couldn't wait for the most important information.

"That would be helpful, thank you," I said. "Can you tell me if it's a boy or a girl, and from which country they'll be transferring?"

"It's a girl who'll be completing the final semester for her senior year. She's transferring in from France."

France, I thought, feeling my heart skip a beat. I'd always wanted to travel there and learn to speak the language, but had never found the time. This would be my chance to learn more about their culture by experiencing it in a whole *different* way.

"That sounds exciting," I said. "When will she be arriving, and are there any final preparation requirements?"

"She's due to arrive January twenty-third, the weekend between first and second semester. The only other preparation requirement is a final in-home interview to ensure you have sufficient accommodation and resources to care for your guest. We can arrange a convenient time to visit next week if that will work for you."

"That's perfect. How about Wednesday at one p.m.? Thank you for keeping me in the queue for consideration with this placement."

"My pleasure, Ms. Robertson. I'll look forward to seeing you next Wednesday. Bye for now."

Later that day, I received the student profile via email. When I opened it, the first thing I saw was a single headshot photo. It was a bit grainy, but she looked pretty and fresh-faced, with wavy blonde hair and bright blue-green eyes. Her name was Luna, and she lived in Saint Denis, a suburb of Paris. She listed her hobbies as yoga, skiing, and dressmaking. Her father was an engineer and her mother was a nurse. She had two siblings, an older sister and a younger brother. Her career interests were international relations and fashion design.

Perfect, I thought. *We can exercise together, go skiing on weekends, and we both have an interest in women's fashion.* It sounded like a match made in heaven.

After successfully passing the home inspection and knowing I'd have a girl as my guest, I went about decorating her room like I was expecting a newborn baby. I went out and bought a new work desk and bookshelf at Ikea and new towels and linens from Bed, Bath, and Beyond. The closer I got to her arrival date, the more excited I became about having my new houseguest. For the next four or five months, I knew my life would never be the same.

2

———

As Luna's arrival date approached, I busied myself tidying up her room, decorating it with girly stuff. I painted the walls pale blue, bought lots of pretty throw pillows, and hung a beautiful photo of the Eiffel Tower to remind her of home. I even picked up a basket of beauty products from the French store L'Occitane, including lavender-scented bubble bath, shea-butter soap, and cherry blossom shampoo and conditioner. I wanted to do everything I could to make her adjustment as smooth as possible.

When her arrival date finally came, I drove with Ms. Laurent from the placement agency to O'Hare airport. While we waited outside the International Arrivals lounge, I tapped my foot nervously, checking my watch every two minutes wondering what was holding her up.

"Shouldn't she be here by now?" I said to Ms. Laurent. "Her flight arrived more than an hour ago."

"This is normal for international arrivals," she said, holding a sign with Luna's name on it as passengers began steaming out of the terminal. "She still has to clear through immigration, pick up her checked bags at the baggage carousel, and find her way through this maze of an airport."

"Does she have your phone number in case she gets lost?"

"Yes, but I'm sure it won't come to that," she said, placing her hand on my forearm, trying to calm me down. "Don't worry, there's only one exit from her arrival terminal, and she was told that we'd be waiting with a sign."

I scanned the swarm of passengers exiting the baggage claim area, trying to recognize her face from the picture in her profile. After another fifteen minutes or so, I saw a young girl throw up her hand and move toward us. When she reached our position, she stood her roller bags on the floor and reached out her hand to Ms. Laurent.

"Madame Laurent?" she said with a lilting French accent.

"Bonjour, Luna," Ms. Laurent said with an equally strong accent. "Comment était votre vol?"

"C'était bien," the girl said, shaking her head in dismay. "Mais c'est un très grand aéroport!"

"Je suis désolé," Ms. Laurent replied. "Je suis content que tu ne t'es pas perdu."

Then the director turned to face me, extending her hand in my direction.

"May I introduce you to your American host, Ms. Jade Robertson?"

"Pleased to meet you, Ms. Robertson," the girl said in perfect English.

"Please, call me Jade," I said, shaking her hand softly as she bent her knees in a gentle curtsy.

I was immediately taken by how beautiful she was up close and in person. She had wavy blond hair with a tinge of red, falling softly over her emerald-green eyes and creamy skin. With her high cheekbones, gently upturned nose and plump, rosebud lips, she looked like a young fashion model straight out of Vogue magazine. Wearing a sheepskin-lined leather bomber jacket overtop skinny jeans and Converse sneakers, I could see how she'd already defined her own unique sense of style.

"Do you need to use the restroom or get something to eat?" Ms. Laurent asked the girl.

"I had a snack on the plane, thank you," she said. "And I found the *toilette* in the baggage claim area."

Even the way she pronounced everyday pedestrian words like toilet in her native tongue was charming. I was already swooning over her, and I'd only met her for a few minutes.

"Can we help you with your bags?" Ms. Laurent said.

"Yes, thank you," the girl said. "I'm really getting a workout juggling these three bags."

Ms. Laurent reached out for the large check bag and I grabbed the smaller carry-on roller while Luna hiked her large tote bag over her shoulder.

"Let's get you situated, then," Ms. Laurent said, pulling the large roller bag in the direction of the ground trans-portation exit door. "Our car isn't parked too far away."

We packed Luna's bags in the trunk of my car, and I invited her to sit in the front passenger seat while Ms. Laurent sat in the back. As we exited the parking garage and pulled onto the 294 ring road heading south, Luna peered out the side window at the passing cityscape of downtown Chicago.

"You live in a very tall city," she said, gazing at the skyscrapers with wide eyes.

"Yes, I suppose it is," I nodded. "But Paris is a large city too. Doesn't it have a lot of skyscrapers also?"

"Very few, and they're all outside the main city. The city

planners banned tall buildings to preserve its unique European flavor. Except for the Eiffel Tower, of course."

"Paris sounds so beautiful," I nodded. "I really must go there soon."

"Perhaps I can return the favor and host you when you visit?" Luna said, peering over at me through long eyelashes.

"That would be lovely," I said, almost missing my exit heading west toward the Naperville suburbs.

"So you live outside the city also?" Luna asked.

"Yes, but I'm only about twenty miles or so from downtown."

"I'm not familiar with miles..."

"That's equivalent to about thirty kilometers," Ms. Laurent chimed in from the back seat.

"Sorry," I said, reaching over to clasp Luna's hand gently. "I'll have to get in the habit of speaking European."

"Not at all," she said. "I'm a guest in your country. It's better that I begin learning about your American culture right away."

When we pulled into my driveway, I removed Luna's bags from the trunk and she peered up at my two-story house.

"What a beautiful home you have, Ms. Roberts—I mean, Jade," she said. "Everything in America is so *big*!"

"Thank you," I smiled. "But this really is just a typical middle-class home here in Chicago. Hopefully, you'll find plenty of room to stretch out. Come, let me show you around."

I escorted Luna and Ms. Laurent through the front door into the foyer, then hung their coats in the closet. Luna was wearing a tight cashmere sweater that matched the color of her eyes, and it took every ounce of my willpower to keep my gaze focused above her prominent, pointy breasts sitting high on her chest. We walked down the hall toward the kitchen, and I placed her bags at the foot of the stairs to the second floor. When she noticed the covered pool in my backyard, she rushed toward the window excitedly.

"You have a *pool* also?" she said. "Ms. Laurent never mentioned that!"

"Unfortunately, it's not much use during the long winter months," I said. "Hopefully we can get it up and running before you head back home." Then I pointed to the hot tub resting in the corner by the exit door. "But I *do* have a Jacuzzi that's quite relaxing on a cold winter day."

"I feel like I'm staying at a luxury hotel," Luna said.

"I wouldn't go that far," I smiled. "But I'm glad you find the accommodations suitable so far."

Ms. Laurent placed her briefcase atop the kitchen island and flipped it open.

"Shall we go over the final arrangements?" she said. "I think it's time you two settled in and begin getting to know one another."

"Certainly," I said. "Why don't you make yourselves comfortable in the living room? Can I get either of you a cup of coffee or tea?"

"Tea will be fine, thank you," Ms. Laurent said.

"Milk and sugar?"

"A little bit of both, thank you."

"Luna?"

"I'll have mine plain, thank you."

Plain it is, I thought, beginning to make a mental note of her preferences. But everything about this girl screamed she was anything but plain.

After I prepared the tea, I brought the cups into the living room and sat down on the sofa next to Luna.

"I've already gone over the protocol with both of you at

some length," Ms. Laurent said. "So I won't bore you with too many more details. I just wanted to reiterate to Luna that as your official stateside sponsor, if you have any questions or concerns at any time, feel free to reach out to me at the number I've provided. That applies equally to you, Ms. Robertson. If you have any questions about legal matters or if any issues arise, please don't hesitate to give me a call."

"I've gone over the care package many times," I said, smiling at Luna as she beamed at me with a slight flush in her cheeks. "Everything looks pretty straightforward. I'm sure Luna and I will get along famously."

Ms. Laurent had us sign the final releases, then she glanced at her phone as it buzzed softly on the coffee table.

"It looks like my taxi is here," she said. "I'll look forward to hearing how you're enjoying your new surroundings, Luna. We'll talk again soon."

After I escorted Ms. Laurent to the front door and watched her pull out of the driveway, I helped Luna carry her bags upstairs to the guest bedroom.

"This is your room," I said, placing her bags by the bed. "I've tried to decorate it with a light feminine touch and some accents from your home country."

Luna peered around the room and smiled when she saw the framed print of the Eiffel Tower.

"It's lovely," she said. "You needn't have gone to so much trouble."

"It's the least I could do for someone visiting America for the first time. Let me show you your bath."

I led her into the washroom across the hall from her room, opening the empty storage lockers.

"Although it isn't attached to your room directly, you'll have the exclusive use of this bathroom. I've cleared out all the cabinets and bought you some toiletries to get you started."

Luna picked up the scented soap in the basket and held it softly under her nose.

"You've gone to so much trouble for me already, Jade," she said, peering up at me through her thick locks of hair. "It's *already* beginning to feel like home."

"I'm glad," I smiled. "Why don't you unpack, then if you'd like, we can go to the supermarket together and get some food for dinner. Or would you prefer to go out to a restaurant?"

"There's no need to treat me any different than any other houseguest," she said. "How does that American expression go? I don't want to eat you out of house and home."

As I watched her bend over to peer inside the shower curtains, I couldn't help staring at her tight, heart-shaped ass.

God forgive me, I said to myself. *Remember, you're her guardian while she's away from home. Get your mind out of the gutter.*

There was something about this precocious French beauty that told me she was going to be much more than just an ordinary houseguest.

3

After Luna finished unpacking, we went to the supermarket together and picked up some food for dinner. I wanted to spoil her on her first day in the U.S., so I baked a prime rib roast with mashed potatoes and gravy, corn on the cob, and apple pie. We chatted about her interests and life experiences, and when I learned that she'd recently turned eighteen, I couldn't help seeing her in a whole new light. She seemed more mature than other girls her age, talking about how the move to a new country to finish out her last year of high school was driven by her desire for independence and to explore new opportunities.

The following day, we went shopping for school supplies, and I got her a new SIM card for her mobile phone so she could make local calls. It was a colder January than usual in Chicago, and when we got home, I invited her to join me in the hot tub. She hadn't packed a swimsuit, and knowing it was too early to invite her to go nude, I offered her my one-piece suit. We were roughly the same dress size, but her waist was definitely narrower and her breasts were firmer and pointier than mine. Before we lowered ourselves into the bubbling water, I admired her tight figure, feeling my pussy throb as the hot liquid enveloped my hips.

"Wow," Luna said, feeling the Jacuzzi jets swirling over her body under the churning water. "You weren't kidding about how relaxing this is. This feels heavenly."

"It's especially nice on a cold winter day," I nodded. "There's something about feeling the hot bubbling water with the cold surrounding air that makes it even more refreshing."

"That, and all these water jets caressing my body," she smiled. "It's like getting a massage from a hundred masseuses."

"You've never enjoyed a hot tub before?" I said, peering at the top of her breasts protruding above the surface of the water as the churning liquid swirled over her erect nipples.

"Not like *this*," she purred, resting her head against her seat rest. "I've had a Jacuzzi bath before, but never outside and never with another person."

I was tempted to tell her about the secret location in the tub where she could receive special stimulation on a different part of her body, but I figured I'd let her discover that for herself another day. It was still early in our relationship, and I didn't want to overstep my role as her host.

"So what do you think of America after your first two days?" I said, changing the subject.

"You mean besides how cold it is in the winter?" she chuckled.

"Sorry about that," I said. "Perhaps you should have looked to relocate to a warmer state like Florida or California."

"Something tells me I'm going to warm up to this place pretty quickly," she said, glancing down at my breasts bobbing atop the swirling water. "Besides, I kind of like the cold weather. My family takes frequent ski trips to the Swiss alps. I don't imagine there's much skiing in Florida or California."

"Florida, no. But you'd be surprised how many ski resorts there are in California. The Sierras get a fair amount of snow in the higher elevations."

"Are there any ski hills near Chicago?"

"There's a few resorts in northern Wisconsin about four hours from here. It's a far cry from the Swiss Alps, but they have passable trails for an intermediate skier."

"I never even thought about bringing my gear with me," Luna said, shaking her head.

"Do you prefer to ski or snowboard?"

"I'm proficient at both, but I'm a slightly better skier."

"Not to worry," I said. "We can rent some equipment at the slopes. Once you get settled in at your new school, we'll make a weekend excursion soon."

"I'd enjoy that very much," Luna nodded, adjusting her position under the swirling water.

"Are you nervous about moving to a new school tomorrow?" I asked.

"Not too much," she said. "I've managed to maintain fairly good grades, and the curriculum between the two school systems is pretty well aligned, so hopefully it won't be too much of any adjustment."

I noticed Luna spreading her arms out to her sides, searching for the new locations of the underwater jets. As she squirmed in her seat, I could tell she was curious to see what they might feel like on other parts of her body, but she was too shy to make such a bold move in my company.

"What about socially?" I asked, eager to see if she had a boyfriend. "Do you make new friends easily?"

"It usually takes me a while to form those kind of bonds,"

she frowned. "Transferring in the middle of the school year doesn't help."

"Well, I'm sure with your pretty looks and charming French accent that it won't take long for you to find new friends." Then I looked at her with an arched eyebrow and a slight curl of my lip. "Is there a special someone back home that you'll miss *especially* much?"

"Not really," Luna smiled, understanding my meaning immediately. "I've been so focused on my studies trying to make sure I get into a good university. I don't have any time for boyfriends."

My pussy twitched when I heard she was unattached. Suddenly, *I* was the one shifting uneasily under the churning water, desperate to feel the jets pulsing against my pussy as I peered at the pretty French girl.

———

Later that evening while Luna checked in with her family back home, I went to my bedroom and propped up my pillows, picking up a book from my nightstand. About a half hour later, I heard her run a bath, and I wondered why she needed to bathe again so soon after our long hot tub. Listening to the sound of her body rubbing against the metal tub while she lowered herself into the water, my mind soon drifted away from the book, imagining what she looked like naked.

I wondered if it was true what they said about French girls not shaving their private areas, and I couldn't stop picturing her pretty tits floating atop the clear water. As much as I enjoyed watching her undulate in the frothy water of the hot tub, I would have killed to be in the bathtub with her right now. After a few minutes, I heard a scraping sound like she was shaving her legs, and I smiled.

So much for European girls going au naturel, I thought. *Apparently, they're just as obsessed as American girls about maintaining their smooth skin.*

I found myself holding my breath as I strained to listen to the sound of the razor scraping her skin and the water sloshing over her naked body as she shifted her position periodically in the tub. After a while, the scraping sound stopped and for a while I couldn't hear anything in the washroom. Then I slowly began to hear the sound of ripples lapping against the side of the tub, and I wondered what she was doing. Straining to listen, I heard her begin to mew as the sound of rippling water began to escalate in pitch and frequency.

Is she...? I thought, suddenly sitting up in my bed.

As her breathing and soft moaning began to grow more noticeable, there was no longer any doubt. She was masturbating in the bathtub!

Now I knew why she wanted to take a bath so soon after our hot tub together. She'd apparently gotten just as aroused as me feeling the swirling water jets caressing her body, and she wanted to re-experience the feeling in the privacy of her own room. I wondered if part of it might *also* have to do with a similarly strong attraction she was feeling for me.

I tiptoed across my carpet and opened my door as wide as it would go, then ripped off my clothes, sitting spread-eagled on my bedspread. As I listened to her soft sighs and moans, I placed my fingers against my clit, surprised at how wet I'd gotten in the last few minutes. While the pleasurable sensations began to spread throughout my body, I closed my eyes imagining what she looked like as she touched herself in the bathtub.

Did she like to squeeze her tits like me when she played with her clit? Did she like to place two fingers inside her pussy and stimulate her G-spot while rubbing her palm against her vulva? Did she have one leg propped up on the side of the bathtub while she jilled herself spread-eagled in the sudsy water? I could almost see the flush spreading over her chest and cheeks as her pleasure escalated in intensity. It didn't take long for the image I was cultivating in my mind to get me so worked up that I experienced a sudden orgasm, squealing softly as I bit my lip.

Suddenly the sloshing sound in the bathroom stopped for a moment as Luna paused to hear what I was doing. While I lay on the bed motionless with my fingers still embedded in my pussy, I felt my heart pounding in my chest as I struggled to slow my breath so Luna wouldn't know what I'd been secretly doing while she touched herself. Then a few moments later, the rhythmic sloshing sound resumed and I heard her moaning and sighing as her body squeaked against the slippery metal surface of the tub.

This time, I remained perfectly still while I curled my fingers softly inside my pussy, listening to Luna's breathing and groans growing more pronounced. Suddenly, I heard a loud splash as she jerked her body forcefully in the tub, and I knew that she'd reached orgasm. Consumed with desire, I began pounding my fingers in and out of my pussy while I tribbed my burning clit with the fingers of my other hand.

This time, my orgasm washed over me like a freight train, and I arched my hips high off the bed, gaping my mouth wide open in the throes of a powerful climax. Trying to stifle my moans, I held my body in an arched position for almost thirty seconds as wave after wave of intense contractions rolled over my body. When I finally collapsed onto my bed, the springs squeaked loudly, and the house became eerily silent.

I wondered if Luna sensed that I'd been pleasuring myself while I listened to her, just as she'd done with me. Either way, something told me there'd be a lot more than just *studying* going on in my household over the next four or five months.

4

———

For the next few weeks, things quieted down as Luna settled in to her new school and concentrated on her studies. We went shopping on weekends, watched movies together on the sofa on weeknights, and enjoyed frequent hot tub dips. But as much as I sensed the burgeoning sexual tension between the two of us, neither of us felt brave enough to make the first move for fear of breaking our unwritten host-student pact.

With the mid-winter school break approaching, I asked Luna if she wanted to head north for a few days of skiing. When she quickly agreed, I booked three nights at a cozy hotel near Granite Peak at Rib Mountain State Park. Luna was an excellent skier, and I had a hard time keeping up with her down the mogul-covered expert trails. In the evenings, we went out for dinner at local restaurants and by the time we returned to the hotel, we were both so exhausted, we fell asleep before ten p.m. But I saw enough of her in her skimpy underwear to have vivid dreams fantasizing about pouncing on top of her on the adjacent bed in our single hotel room. By the time we headed back home, I felt our relationship had reached a new level of comfort and closeness.

"Did you enjoy our little getaway?" I said, peering over at Luna as she stared out her window on the drive home.

"Yes, thank you so much, Jade," she said, turning to face me with a big smile. "You're the best host I could have ever hoped for. Sometimes I feel like I've hardly left home. Between the ski trips, restaurants, shopping, and everything else, you've made me feel like part of your family."

"Everything but the *hot tubs*, right?" I grinned.

"I have to admit, that's a lovely perk," she nodded. "Although with the weather beginning to warm up, we might not have so much need for it soon."

"In another month or so we can look into opening up the pool. It's heated too, so maybe you'll find it just as relaxing and refreshing on cool evenings and weekends."

"I'll have to look into getting my own swim suit soon," she smiled. "I'm going to wear yours out pretty soon with all the use it gets in the hot tub."

"Now that you *mention* that," I said, peering over at her. "I've been thinking. You've told me about your dressmaking hobby and your interest in exploring fashion design as a potential career. I'd like to buy you a sewing machine so you'll have something else to do with your free time."

"I could never expect you to buy me such an expensive gift," Luna said, shaking her head. "You've already spent far too much paying for the hotel and the restaurants on this ski trip."

"Hey, I enjoyed those just as much as *you* did. Besides, I've been wanting to get a sewing machine for myself for some time now. They're not that expensive, and I'll get almost as much use out of it after you've gone as you will."

"Only if you *promise* to use it after I leave," Luna said,

peering at me earnestly. Then her expression changed as her eyes opened wide and her forehead wrinkled in delight. "Maybe we can have some fun designing and making patterns *together*!"

"I'd really enjoy that, Luna. We still have a few days left in the winter holiday. Would you like to go to the fabric store tomorrow and look around for ideas?"

"That would be awesome!" Luna said, bouncing up and down excitedly on her car seat. "Oh my God—you're the *best*, Jade!"

T he following day, we set out to the local fabric store to begin searching for material. We both agreed that we'd like to surprise each other with our initial designs, so we paid for our samples separately then we went home and began sketching some ideas. After supplying each other with our measurements, we set out crafting our garments. With Luna's measurements of 35-23-34, I wanted to make something sexy and flattering for her figure. While *she* worked in the evenings and on weekends on her design, I worked during the day while she was at school.

When the day finally came to reveal our designs to each other, we met in the living room like two kids at Christmas. We did rock-paper-scissors to see who would go first, and Luna won the first round.

"Okay," she said excitedly to me. "I've got your item wrapped up in this garment bag, so I want you to turn around before I reveal it."

"Now you've got *me* all excited," I said, turning around to face the windows looking out into the backyard. "Tell me when it's okay to turn around."

I heard Luna unzip her garment bag, followed by a slight rustling sound, then she giggled softly.

"Okay, I'm ready," she said.

I turned around and peered at a cream-colored linen mid-length dress with cropped sleeves and a small slit on each side of the lower hem.

"Wow," I said, widening my eyes. "It looks *gorgeous*! Can I try it on?"

"Absolutely," Luna smiled with a huge grin.

"Do you mind if I undress here?"

"It's just us girls," she nodded with a smile. "No one else is looking."

I kicked off my loafers then pulled my pants down and unzipped my blouse, laying them over the back edge of the sofa. Then I unzipped the back closure and stepped into the dress wearing only a bra and panties. The dress fit snuggly over my hips and ass, and the V-neck top hugged my bosom perfectly, creating a slim, tapered look.

"Can you zip me up in the back?" I said, turning around.

For the first time, I felt Luna's hands caress my bare skin as she closed the panels and zipped them together. I turned around to face her, feeling my nipples getting hard and my panties moistening.

"It fits perfectly," I gushed, swiping my hands down the side of the dress, stepping forward to see how much room I had to maneuver. "And the little side slits leave just enough room to move around comfortably. You absolutely *nailed* this one, Luna. How did you know linen was one of my favorite fabrics?"

Luna looked at me sheepishly and shrugged.

"I confess that I peeked in your closet when you weren't looking to get some ideas. I hope you like it."

"I love it!" I said. "It's classic, sexy, and timeless. Though I might not be able to wear it until summer. Because of that silly no-white-before-Memorial-Day rule."

"At least I'll see it on you before I leave," Luna smiled. "I was hoping you might also wear it when you come to visit me in France this summer."

"I'd love that Luna," I smiled, leaning in to kiss her on the cheek.

"Why don't you go for a walk down the hall to see how comfortably it moves with you?"

"Okay," I said, strutting down the hall using my best supermodel catwalk imitation, swinging my hips from side to side in an exaggerated manner as I stepped one foot in front of the other.

"Wow," Luna said. "It almost looks better from *behind* than from the front, if you don't mind my saying. Is there enough room for you to walk comfortably?"

"Absolutely," I said, swinging around and affecting a pouty model face as I strode back down the hall toward her. "There's just enough play in the skirt with the side slits to allow me to walk with a normal gait. This is the absolute perfect dress! Thank you, Luna, for making me such a pretty garment. You really do have a knack for this."

"The pleasure was all mine," Luna beamed. "But with a figure like yours, I suspect even a *potato sack* would look good on you."

"Hardly," I said. "But it's my turn now. Turn around while I get your surprise ready."

"Okay," Luna squeaked, barely able to contain herself as she turned to face the windows overlooking the backyard.

I pulled her two-piece garment out of a department store bag and held them up, one on top of the other.

"Okay," I said, excited to reveal my design. "You can turn around now."

When Luna flipped around and saw what I'd made, her eyes flew open and she jumped up and down excitedly.

"Oh my God–they're *beautiful!*" she exclaimed, moving in closer to examine the lacy camisole and matching silk shorts.

"I hope you don't think I was being too forward designing a sexy loungewear set for you," I said. "But I thought these would look beautiful on you and now that you're almost finished high school, I thought you might like something to make you feel all grown up."

"Are you *kidding* me?" she said. "I've always dreamed of owning something like this, but my parents would never let me wear them."

She stepped forward and pinched the fabric between her fingers, rubbing it softly.

"Is this...?"

"Yes," I smiled. "It's real silk. None of that fake polyester Victoria's Secret stuff for my pretty European model. I wanted to make a first-class outfit for a first-class girl."

"Can I try them on?" she said.

"Of course. That is, if you feel comfortable taking your clothes off–"

Luna practically ripped off her jeans and t-shirt then unclasped her bra and pulled down her panties, throwing them in a pile next to mine on the sofa. Seeing her for the first time naked, I couldn't help but glance down at her exquisite figure. Her breasts sat high and proud on her chest, pointing straight out like a Madonna corset, with large brown areolas and pink nubs. Her mound was shaved perfectly bald, and my mind suddenly wandered back to the memory of listening to her shaving in the bathtub while my pussy fluttered under my linen dress.

She pulled on the silky shorts first, then she lifted her

arms as I watched the camisole slide down over her shoulders and her protruding tits. I was worried about getting the fit right over her uniquely shaped breasts, but when the straps fell over her shoulders, the fabric draped sexily over her mounds with just the right amount of cling and loose folds. And the lacy top hem swept down just enough to tastefully show off her tight cleavage without making it look trampy.

"How do I look?" Luna said, smiling at me sexily.

"*Mouth-watering*," I said, feeling my panties growing damper by the moment. "You could give any one of those Victoria Secret models a run for their money. How's the fit?"

"It clings to my body with just the right amount of drape. And the silk feels absolutely heavenly against my bare skin. Do you mind if I see what it looks like in your upstairs dressing mirror?"

"Of course," I said, taking her hand and leading her toward the stairs. "I was thinking the same thing."

When we got to my bedroom, Luna stepped in front of the full-length mirror and gasped. The soft baby-blue with cream-colored lace accents made her look sexy and innocent at the same time. While she peered at the front profile of her lingerie set, I ran my eyes over her tight ass perfectly framed by the clingy silk fabric.

"It fits me perfectly!" she gushed, twisting her body from side to side while she peered at herself in front of the mirror. "How does it look from behind?"

"Just as sexy as from the *front*," I smiled. "See for yourself."

Luna turned her body around then twisted her head to look at her reflection in the mirror.

"How did you get it to fit me so perfectly?" she said,

pushing her butt out in a vampy pose. "It fits every curve of my body like a glove!"

"I've had a fair amount of time to study your body in my wet swimsuit in the hot tub these past few weeks. Your figure is indelibly imprinted on my brain."

"Thank you, Jade," Luna said, rushing up toward me and flinging her arms around my neck while she pressed her tits and hips against me.

As I hugged her softly, I desperately wanted to place my hand under her chin and kiss her, pulling her onto the bed only a few inches away. But somehow I managed to keep it together and release her after a few moments, while we continued admiring our fashion designs in the mirror.

If this was the best way to get her body pressing up against mine, I thought, I was already thinking of the *next* clothing design I had in mind for her.

5

—————

Over the next few weeks, Luna and I continued to make increasingly sexy outfits for one another. My next design was a cut-out one-piece swimsuit with a large oval opening on both sides of her midsection that accentuated her curvy figure. For her part, she designed a matching lace bra and panty ensemble that took my lingerie set one step further. Feeling excited about carrying our mutual clothing design venture to the next level, I left a message for her on the fridge one afternoon while I went to the fabric store to shop for more material.

Luna,

Running some errands this afternoon. Should be home around 5:00 p.m. Feel like pizza tonight?

Jade

I received a text back from her when she got home from school saying pizza sounded great, but by then I'd finished most of my shopping so I headed back a bit earlier than planned. When I pulled into the driveway, I didn't open the garage door like usual because I wanted to sneak my new fabric design in without her seeing it. Opening the door softly, I tiptoed down the hall and up the stairs, hoping to hide the material in my closet.

But as I approached my bedroom, I heard a soft buzzing sound and I paused at the partially closed door, peering through the crack. Luna was lying buck naked on my bed with a vibrator humming loudly between her legs. I recognized it immediately as my Rabbit vibrator and she was holding the end of it with two hands while she pressed the flapping ears tightly against her pussy.

Instantly aroused in a fit of passion, I placed the fabric bag down on the floor and unzipped my pants, thrusting my fingers under my soaking panties. As I watched Luna ramming the dildo in and out of her bare cunny, I trilled my clit rapidly, feeling my knees beginning to weaken. She looked even *more* beautiful with a soft flush filling her face and her pointy tits jiggling on her chest as she rolled her hips and flexed her arms, fucking herself with the buzzing vibrator.

As she began to arch her back and widen her mouth in mounting ecstasy, it took every ounce of my willpower not to barge through the door and take her into my arms. The more she tensed her body and arched her back, the closer my own orgasm steamrolled toward me. When she suddenly grunted and began jerking her body forward and back in the midst of a powerful orgasm, I felt my juices spraying all over my hand and jeans resting halfway down my thighs.

I was tempted to sneak away before she caught me lurking outside the door, but there was something about seeing the girl I'd fantasized about for the past two months naked on my bed that kept me hesitating in the hall. After she recovered from her orgasm, she pulled the still-buzzing Rabbit vibrator out of her pussy. Seeing her juices glistening on the whirring contraption made my pussy throb as two more steams of lubrication trickled down the inside of my thighs. When she reached over and pulled open my nightstand drawer to search for another toy, I smiled.

That's it, baby, I purred. *Go ahead and try out my entire collection. Give your momma a nice show.*

When she lifted the oversize Magic Wand vibrator out of the drawer, my heart fluttered.

You better be careful with that one, sweetie. It packs a hellova punch.

This was one of the few vibrators I owned that had a power cord, and Luna lifted herself off the bed, searching for the nearest outlet. While I watched her bend over, revealing the glistening slit between her legs as she plugged the device into the wall, I kicked off my jeans and panties, eager to free up my pussy for less restricted access. Something told me this show might go on for a while, and I planned on enjoying it to the fullest. But when she climbed back on the bed instead of lying back down face up, she surprised me by getting on all fours with her bare ass pointed directly in my direction.

Fuck me, I thought to myself. *You're making this damn near impossible for me, girl.* Now it was going to be even more difficult to restrain myself from barging through the door and pouncing on top of her.

As I watched her spread her knees apart then rest her chest on the bed as she angled her hips up in the air, I stood mesmerized outside the door. I could see her entire gleaming vulva from her bald pubis down over her splayed lips, all the way to her tight brown pucker. Even her swollen clit was visible from my position, poised like a ripe cherry at the junction of her folds under the bottom of her mound.

Oh, how I longed to be lying between her legs, taking her plump fruit into my mouth.

But when she flicked on the big vibrator and positioned the pulsating ball over her erect gland, I lost all sense of space and time. As her hips began to undulate against the vibrating head, I thrust three fingers inside my pussy and began fucking myself hard. I could see her tits hanging between the A-frame of her splayed legs, and when she grabbed one breast with her other hand and began squeezing it while she moaned in pleasure, I unbuttoned my own blouse and thrust my bra up under my neck, pinching my nipples.

I hadn't witnessed such an erotic sight in a very long time, and I bit my lip trying to remain silent while I watched the sexy nymph pleasuring herself. As I watched her juices pouring out of her snatch and rolling down the insides of her thighs, I could hear her cries and whimpers growing in urgency. But when she reached around behind her ass with her free hand and thrust two fingers into her pussy while she rocked back and forth on the bed, I almost lost it. I had to stop fingering myself for fear of falling off the cliff and making a commotion.

Besides, I wanted to save myself for the big finish. I wanted to dream that I was right there *with* her, grinding my sopping pussy against her while we came together.

As Luna began pumping her fingers harder into her hole, she turned her head sideways on the bed, and I saw the look of ecstasy on her face. As she opened her mouth wider approaching another orgasm, I suddenly felt my cunt clamping down on my fingers as I jetted my juices all over my palm. Seconds later, Luna emitted a loud squeal as she pulled her fingers out of her cunny and I saw her rosebud contracting in powerful convulsions while she pressed the vibrating ball of the magic wand hard against the base of her mound.

Oh my God, I panted outside my door, trying to control my breathing so as not to be heard.

Thinking that would be the end of it, I was surprised a few minutes later when Luna peered inside the drawer one more time then pulled out my favorite sex toy, the Osé vibrator. Designed to mimic the movement of a person's natural anatomy, the uniquely shaped device had a long bulbous finger-shaped projection that curled forward in rhythmic pulses to stimulate the front side of a woman's G-spot. The other part of the device had a small opening in the base with a flexible tongue designed to imitate the action of a person's mouth. When it was fully inserted into the vagina, the two parts together delivered an unforgettable experience unlike anything else, designed to give its recipient a blended, full-body orgasm.

Luna peered at the device with pinched eyebrows for a moment, turning it over in her hands trying to figure out how the various parts worked. Eventually, she found the power button on the base of the unit, and when she held it down I saw a small green LED light illuminate.

That's my girl, I smiled. *It takes a little getting used to, but if you just play with the buttons enough, you'll figure it out.*

Flipping the device upside-down, she noticed the control buttons under the base. She pressed one of the buttons, then her eyes lit up as the finger-shaped appendage began flexing toward her in a come-hither motion. When she pressed the little plus symbol next to the button, the finger began moving more rapidly. Shaking her head in shock, she ramped down the speed of the finger then tapped the other button. Suddenly, the aperture at the base of the unit began to pucker open and shut, mimicking the motion of a moving mouth. Luna leaned her head closer to the device, mesmerized by the strange object.

Pretty incredible, right? I muttered, teleporting my thoughts to her through the thin crack in the door. *You have no idea how heavenly it feels until you actually put it inside you.*

She turned all the power functions off, then sat up against my headboard with her knees hiked up toward her chest. Then she slowly inserted the long finger into her slit until the base was pressed firmly against her vulva. When she tapped the finger-control button on the base of the unit and felt it moving inside her, she groaned softly.

"Yes, Jade," she purred. "Finger my pussy while I look at your beautiful body."

I stepped away from the door, wondering if she'd seen my shadow moving in the hall. But when I peered back at her, her eyes were closed as she continued talking to herself. When she tapped the clitoral-control button, she slid her hips down while spreading her knees further apart.

"Oh God, Jade," she moaned. "That feels incredible. Lick my clit with your soft tongue. I want to feel your face against my pussy when I come."

Holy shit, I thought, plunging my fingers back into my dripping hole. *She's fantasizing about the device being my own fingers and mouth touching her instead of the artificial toy!*

Knowing she wanted me as much as I'd fantasized about having her, ratcheted up my pleasure tenfold as my juices began flowing out of my pussy in rivers. I was tempted to swing open the door and tell her I was waiting right here for her, but I didn't want to invade her privacy and embarrass her using my toys. I'd have to wait for another time to make my first move. But right now, I was going to *enjoy* this fantasy show to the fullest.

As she began to undulate her hips against the throbbing device, Luna tapped the plus button on the base of the unit, increasing the speed and intensity of the two simultaneous functions. Holding the base of the unit tightly against her snatch, she grabbed one of her tits with her other hand and moaned loudly.

"Fuck yes," she grunted. "Suck my clit while you finger my cunt, Jade. You feel so good, I'm going to come soon all over your face..."

Yes please, I hissed, watching her fuck herself with the animatronic device. My juices were now dripping all over my hand and my pants lying on the floor below my legs, and I wondered how I was going to put them back on and sneak past her without her knowing what I'd been doing.

"Jade!" she suddenly squealed. "I'm going to come. I'm going to come so hard all over your pretty face. Make me–*unghhh!*"

When I saw Luna climaxing again with the sexy toy embedded in her pussy, I watched her face contorted in sweet agony, wishing it was my face planted between her knees instead of the artificial vibrator. As her body quivered and writhed on the bed in the midst of another powerful climax, I clenched my jaw trying to control my breathing, pursing my lips to make sure she couldn't hear my own suppressed squeaks. It was most powerful orgasm I'd experienced in months, and it took almost a full minute for my contractions to stop pulsing inside me.

When I finally stopped shaking outside the door, Luna suddenly turned her wrist to look at her watch, then she got up off the bed and dashed into the washroom to clean off the vibrators. I looked at my phone, and realizing it was approaching five o'clock, I pulled up my pants and crept back downstairs. Then I quietly opened the front door and waited outside on the doorstep for a few minutes to allow Luna to put herself back together.

After three or four minutes, I opened the door with a flourish and called Luna's name to announce myself.

"Hello beautiful," I shouted. "I'm home. Are you hungry?"

I smiled listening to her scampering upstairs as she ran from my bedroom into her own. It looked like the two of us were going to continue our little cat-and-mouse game for a little longer. Holding the fabric store shopping bag in front of my crotch as I ascended the stairs to conceal the giant wet stain on the front of my jeans, I scurried into my room and changed into fresh clothes. After I stowed the shopping bag in my closet and washed the smell of my juices off my hands, I went downstairs and saw Luna sitting on the sofa watching TV like nothing had happened.

"How was your day today?" I asked, pressing my lips together to conceal my knowing smile.

"Pretty uneventful," Luna replied. "You?"

"I picked up some more material at the fabric store. I can't wait for you to see what I've got planned for my next surprise."

"I like surprises," Luna said, peering back at me from the sofa.

"Me too," I smiled. "Are you hungry?"

"Voracious," she said. "I could eat a horse."

That's not the only thing I could eat right now, I thought, gazing back at her like a Cheshire Cat.

6

———

For the next week or so, the sexual tension in the house continued to ramp up as Luna took more frequent baths, making little effort to conceal her increasingly noisy self-pleasuring activity. One day, not long after school ended, I came home from a shopping trip and saw her lying in the hot tub with a more flushed face than usual. As I began putting the groceries away in the cupboards, I glanced at her in the reflection of the microwave glass panel and noticed that she was positioned in the special spot where she could receive direct underwater stimulation to her private areas.

I turned around and motioned to her that I was coming out to join her, and she waved for me to come in. But this time, I didn't even bother going through the pretense of changing into a bathing suit as I stripped off my clothes and scampered out the back door, lowering my naked body into the swirling water.

"I hope you don't mind if I enjoy the hot tub in the *nude* this time," I said. "I think we've seen each naked enough times by now that there shouldn't be any more surprises."

"Of course not," she smiled. "I was thinking the same thing. Though I have to admit I've been enjoying wearing this sexy new swimsuit you made for me."

"Are you finding the openings in the fabric provide enough stimulation from the underwater jets?"

"Yes," she said, subtly adjusting her position on the seat. "Although sometimes I wish there were a few *other* strategically placed holes for me to fully appreciate this experience."

"I know what you mean," I smiled. "I see you've found the special spot in the tub where you can receive an even *more* invigorating massage."

"It's pretty hard to miss," Luna nodded, spreading her legs wider apart under the churning water. "Is there a similar spot on the other side of the tub where you can enjoy it too?"

"As a matter of fact, there *is*," I grinned, positioning my pussy directly in front of the underwater jet shooting up from the base of the tub. "*Mmm*–that feels better."

"You seem to have quite a few toys in the household for stimulating your body," she smiled.

"How do you mean?" I asked coyly. "Like *what* other toys?"

"Um..." Luna hesitated as a deep flush rolled over her face.

"It's okay," I said. "I know that you found my secret stash of sex toys. I saw you using them one day when I came home a bit early."

"You don't mind?"

"Are you kidding me?" I said. "I enjoyed watching you almost as you did *using* them."

"Well now that we're not sharing secrets anymore," Luna smiled. "I heard you out in the hall that day. I enjoyed giving you a little show, hoping you might come in and join me on the bed."

"Oh, Luna," I gushed, feeling the powerful jet spraying against my tingling clit. "I've wanted you from the minute I first saw you–"

"The feeling was mutual," Luna said, looking me squarely in my eyes as her own pleasure beginning to escalate from the jet caressing her covered vulva.

She pulled her hands out of the water and stripped off her swimsuit, throwing it on the deck of the hot tub.

"Fuck it," she said. "No more playing around. I'm going to enjoy this hot tub the way it was intended. I want to come this time watching you orgasm with me."

"Yes, baby," I panted. "Come with me while I watch you. I'm already close."

"I'm coming, Jade," Luna suddenly grunted as her eyes glazed over.

"Uhnnn," I groaned, gazing at her as we both shuddered under the swirling water.

We watched our heads bobbing in spastic union for a few moments, then we both smiled.

"That took a lot longer to happen than I planned," I said.

"Why don't we go upstairs and *finish* this properly?" Luna smiled. "It's about time I felt your soft skin against me instead of these artificial jets or a silicone sex toy."

"Are you sure you want to do this?" I said, hardly believing my own ears. "I mean, we'd be overstepping the bounds of our arrangement..."

"We're both adults," Luna said. "What Ms. Laurent and my parents don't know won't hurt them. I need you so bad. Please make love to me, Jade."

"You're twisting my arm," I said. "But just to be sure the neighbors don't get suspicious, why don't you put your swimsuit back on before you get out of the tub? I'll join you in a few minutes after I make sure the coast is clear."

"Good idea," Luna said, pulling the suit off the deck and squeezing her body back into it under the cover of the water. "I'll be waiting for you in your bed upstairs."

The next two minutes seemed like an eternity as I thought about my sexy angel waiting for me naked and dripping wet. After a short waiting period, I glanced around me at the surrounding yards to make sure nobody was watching, then I scampered out of the hot tub and ran upstairs, not even bothering to dry off. When I saw Luna spread out naked on my bed with the covers pulled down, I jumped on the mattress next to her, wrapping my arms and legs tightly around her.

"Luna," I panted, feeling electrified from the sensation of her warm body next to mine. "I can't believe we're finally going to do this. I've waited so long..."

"Me too," Luna purred, pressing her hips and breasts against mine. "I always wondered what it would be like to make love to a woman. And I can't imagine a more perfect partner. I've grown very close to you these past few months."

"Oh baby," I sighed. "I feel exactly the same way. I haven't felt like this in such a long time."

"Is this your first time with a woman also?" she asked.

"No," I smiled. "But it's the first time with another woman I've felt so close to."

"Make love to me, Jade," she purred. "I want to feel your love as you caress me."

"Yes, baby," I said. "I'm going to love every square inch of your body."

I inserted my thigh between her legs and pulled it up toward her crotch, feeling her slippery lubrication coating the inside of her thighs. When I pressed my leg against her pussy, she moaned, thrusting her tongue into my mouth while we kissed each other passionately.

"Mmm," she hummed. "You feel so soft. I want to feel you *everywhere*."

"Oh you *will* baby," I said, edging myself lower down her body.

When I reached her neck, I nibbled on her skin then sucked her flesh into my mouth.

"I thought we were supposed to be careful about letting people know what we've been up to?" she said. "You're going to leave hickeys all over me!"

"Who's to say they were from *me*?" I smiled. "You're a big girl now. Isn't this what teenagers do to each other behind the portables at school?"

"You're very bad, Jade," Luna panted.

"You have *no* idea," I said.

Feeling her tits caressing the sides of my neck, I moved my face lower, swirling my tongue over her beautiful brown medallions while I sucked her erect nipples into my mouth with a loud popping sound. I'd dreamed of sucking her tits ever since I saw her in her tight sweater. Feeling her finally in my soft, pliant mouth was driving me insane with desire, and I could feel my juices coating her thighs as I rubbed my body against her. I lifted my face and squeezed her tits with my hands, kneading the firm flesh between my fingers.

"You have no idea how much I've wanted to touch you like this," I said, blowing softly on her puckering teats.

"Oh, I have an idea," she groaned. "Between the sexy lingerie set you designed for me and the cutaway swimsuit, you seemed to be overly focused on my girl parts."

"You got that right," I said. "Do you mind if I take a moment to fulfill one particular fantasy I've been harboring ever since I saw these beautiful breasts up close and personal?"

"I can't imagine what you're thinking," Luna smiled. "But I want you to do everything a woman can do to another woman in the remaining time we have together. I don't ever want to forget this time we have left."

I lifted my body up and knelt over her torso with my knees straddling her chest, then I lowered my dripping pussy onto one of her tits. When she felt my warm vulva touching her skin, she reached down and grabbed her breast with two hands, rolling it back and forth over my throbbing slit.

"Oh *God*, Luna," I panted, feeling her erect nipple pressing into my opening. "Fuck me with your beautiful breasts. That feels incredible."

"This is way better than playing with a *sex toy*," she said, smiling up at me.

"Even that special *white* one with the bendy finger and realistic tongue action?"

"There's no comparison," she said. "You're softer, warmer, and wetter. And besides, you can't make *love* to a sex toy, even one that imitates human movement so well."

"Oh, Luna," I said, bending forward to kiss her. "I've fallen in love with you these past few months. I don't ever want you to leave."

"Let's enjoy the little time we have together to the fullest," she smiled. "We have a lot of catching up to do."

"Mmm," I said, rolling my sopping pussy all over her firm mounds. "You feel so good, baby. Keep tribbing me with your tits."

As Luna flapped her breast against my quivering pussy, I moaned louder and louder into her mouth, rapidly approaching my peak. Sensing I was getting close, Luna grabbed the sides of my hips, slowing my movement.

"Can I feel you come in my *mouth* instead this first time?" she asked. "I want to watch your face while I kiss you in your most intimate place. This has been *my* fantasy these past few months."

"As long as you let me return the favor," I said, lifting my head and gazing into her eyes. "Are you sure you're going to know how to do this?"

"How hard can it be?" she smiled. "I'll just imitate the action of the Osé sex toy that I used while you were watching me a few days ago."

"Mmm," I nodded. "I've come many times imagining that was another woman's mouth on my pussy. But something tells me this time it's going to be a hundred times better."

"Only a *hundred*?" Luna smirked.

"Come here," I said, shimmying my hips overtop of her head and lowering my steaming cunt onto her rosebud lips. "Suck my pussy with those pretty lips."

"Mmmm," Luna moaned, feeling my erect nub in her mouth as I coated her face with the juices streaming out of my slit.

She looked up at me and grabbed both of my tits with her two hands, squeezing them firmly. Seeing her pretty face framed by my thighs straddling her head drove me crazy, and when we locked eyes expressing how close we felt to one another at that moment, a tear rolled down my cheek.

"Luna," I groaned. "I love you, baby. It won't take me long now. Can I come on your sweet, beautiful face?"

"*Mm-hmm*," Luna nodded excitedly, squeezing my tits with three quick pulses to show that she returned the sentiment.

"Here's it comes, baby," I gushed. "Oh God, I'm *cumming. Nnngh!*"

As my orgasm washed over me, my entire body began shaking as I gushed all over Luna's flushed cheeks. She blinked her eyes in surprise but never stopped caressing my clit as she sucked it tightly in her mouth. While I sat convulsing over her face, she peered up at me with her aquamarine eyes, cupping my breasts lovingly in her hands. When I finally finished coming, I lifted myself off her and lay down next to her, tasting my juices on her lips as I intertwined my tongue with hers.

"That was *incredible*," I said, pulling back to look into her eyes.

"Was I okay for my first time?"

"*Okay*?" I said, widening my eyes. "You're a natural at this. Now I'm going to miss you all the more when you leave. Nothing's going to make up for you being gone."

"Not even that special rabbit vibrator with the rotating shaft and the flapping ears?"

"Not even *that*," I laughed, leaning in to kiss her again. "But it's your turn now. I've been dreaming about touching *another* part of your body for quite a while. It's time for me to taste *you* and feel you come in my mouth now."

"I'd like that," Luna smiled. "But we've still got a few days to explore each other's bodies. Can you *hold* me when you make love to me this time? I want to feel *every* part of you rubbing up against me when we come together."

"*God* yes," I said. "You've been reading my mind."

I rolled Luna onto her back then lifted myself on top of her, straightening my legs between hers as I pressed my pubis against her mound. She lifted her knees and spread her legs apart as she angled her hips upward, pressing her wet vulva against mine. We both moaned and grabbed each other's heads, pulling our lips together. As our tongues danced in each other's mouths, we began to rock our hips in unison. I could feel Luna's tits pressing against mine, and my entire body tingled from the sensation of her rubbing up against me.

She rocked her hips awkwardly against mine, trying to lock our pussies together, but in our missionary position it was difficult to get traction on both of our clits. I lifted my body and moved up a few inches, straddling her stomach with my thighs, then I pressed my sex down over her bald mound. She spread her legs further apart at the same time, tilting her hips upward until our glands touched. When she felt my hard clit rubbing against hers, she groaned deeply into my mouth, pressing her fingers into my back.

As we began to hump each other, I could hear the sound of our wet pussies smacking together while our juices rolled down the insides of both our thighs. Feeling her warm flesh pressed against mine was everything I'd dreamed of, and it didn't take long for me to feel the familiar pangs of a powerful orgasm rising within me again.

"Luna," I panted. "I've wanted to feel you like this for so long. I'm going to come soon. Let me feel you come *with* me while I hold you in my arms."

"Yes, Jade," Luna grunted. "I feel so close to you. Oh *God!*"

Suddenly she dug her nails hard into my back as she squeezed my hips tightly with her thighs, grunting loudly into my mouth. Feeling her hot pussy against mine when she came soon pushed me also over the edge also, as I sprayed my juices all over her gaping hole while I pressed my cunt hard against her. As we both squealed and groaned into each other's mouths, I held her tightly until we finished coming. When we finally finished quivering in each other's arms, I lay down beside her, softly stroking her cheek as I gazed into her eyes.

"Do you know what we French girls call an orgasm?" she said, smiling at me.

"I have no idea," I said, shaking my head.

"We call it *la petite mort*," she said. "It means little death."

"That's funny," I chuckled. "I guess that's kind of fitting, given all the convulsions we experience at the moment of climax and the way we go limp afterwards. But that reminds me. I haven't spent nearly as much time as I'd hoped learning your language while you've been with me. There's so much more I was hoping you could teach me."

"I'll be happy to," Luna said, suddenly rolling back on top of me. "But something tells me you've still got plenty to teach me too."

As our bodies melded back together again, I couldn't help smiling. This cultural exchange program had been far more beneficial for both of us than I'd ever imagined.

Everybody's an exhibitionist in disguise

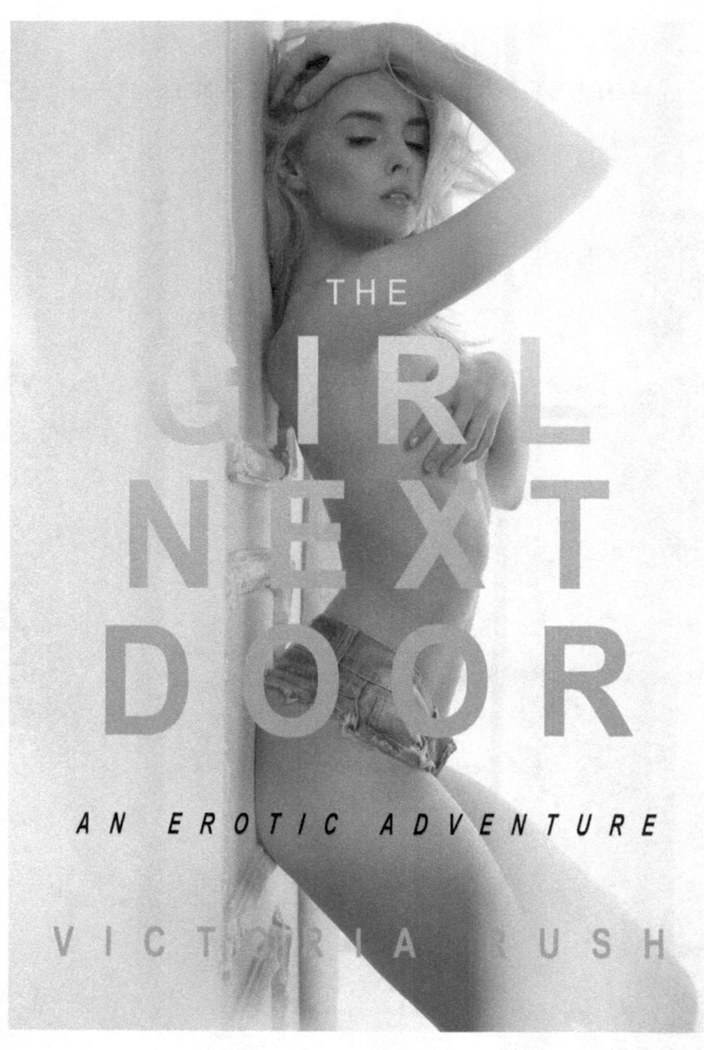

Spying on the neighbors just got a lot more interesting...

Everything's sexier in the dark...

NUDE CRUISE

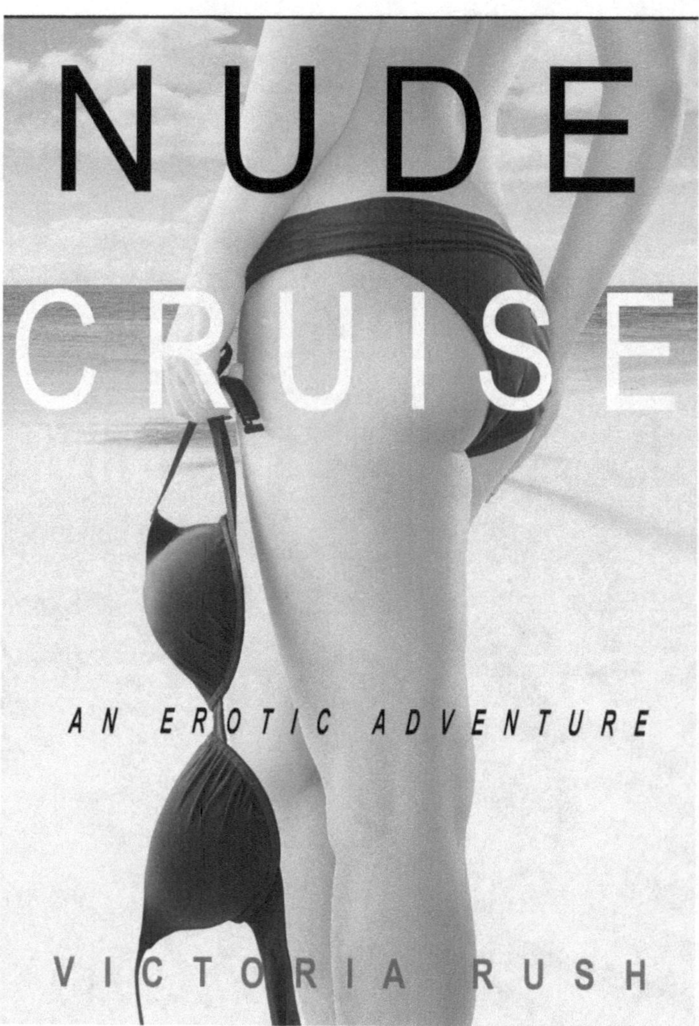

Some people get wet on a cruise for different reasons...

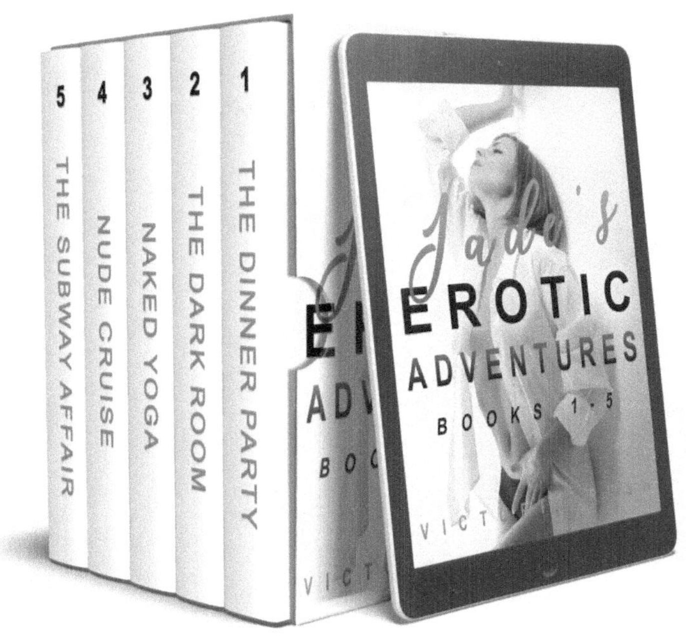

Books 1 -5 in the bestselling erotica series - 60% off

"Okay, so now that I'm committed, tell me where you had in mind for this little experiment."

"Actually," Hannah said, "I have a *series* of places in mind, each one more challenging than the one before."

"But I thought you said this was a one-off proposition?"

"I said nothing of the sort. I only said that if you won, I'd pay for the flights to Bora Bora. If you want me to cover the cost of hotels, food, and all the other incidentals, you'll have to pass progressively tougher tests. We don't want to make this *too* easy for you, do we?"

I crossed my arms and huffed, putting on my best pouty face.

"It hardly seems fair," I said. "But I'm still game. Besides, either one of us can pull out at any time to lock in our gains, right?"

"I suppose so," Hannah shrugged. "But what would be the fun in that? Something tells me once you've tried the first experiment, you won't want to stop. I think you're going to find this whole thing quite titillating and exciting. This will be the most fun either one of us has had in a long time."

I pushed the rest of my half-eaten salmon dish to the side, suddenly no longer interested in eating.

"Okay, lay it on me then. Where are you planning to take me for the first test?

Hannah gulped down the rest of her margarita then peered at me with a lopsided grin.

"Church. More specifically, a *Catholic* church. You haven't been in quite a while, have you? This will be your chance to repent and atone for all your sins."

"It's not like I've broken any commandments or anything–"

"The Catholic Church still considers sex outside of marriage a mortal sin. So technically, you've been doing a ton of sinning since your marriage ended."

"Well I haven't been a practicing Catholic for ages," I snorted. "So my conscience is clear. This'll be a cakewalk. All I have to do is sit quietly in my pew, right?"

"Yes, but it'll be a *front-row* pew, in full view of the priest who'll be delivering the sermon."

"Okay, but I'll be fully clothed, right? It's not like there'll be anything for him to see..."

"Not if you can keep your composure and don't cum all over the floor," Hannah said, cocking her head playfully.

"I don't think I'll have any difficulty keeping my dick in my pants, in a manner of speaking. But you raise a good point. You can't expect me not to get a little wet while you're stimulating me. What will I be allowed to wear?"

"I assume you'll dress appropriately, wearing your Sunday best. A mid-length skirt and button-up blouse should do the trick. You should be able to hide a few dribbles that way, right?"

"I suppose so, but how will we muffle the sound of the vibrator buzzing inside my panties? There's likely to be other people sitting around me in adjacent pews..."

"Never fear," Hannah smiled, reaching into her purse and pulling out a U-shaped silicone sex toy. "I've been talking with our friend at the local Babeland store. She's given me the latest prototype of the We-Vibe vibrator to test." She held up a smaller device with two control buttons and a flywheel. "Complete with a Bluetooth remote control. And the best thing is that it's whisper-quiet.

"Here," she said, handing me the flexible device. "See for yourself."

She tapped one of the buttons on the remote and the thick side of the contraption began buzzing softly in my hand.

"Okay," I nodded, looking around me to see if any other restaurant patrons were distracted by the gentle hum of the object. "It's *quiet* enough, but which end goes inside?"

"The bulbous end is a natural G-spot stimulator. You place the flatter end against your clit, then pull the thing up tight against your vulva to keep it snugly in place."

I suddenly became mindful of the wetness permeating my panties as I imagined the device vibrating inside me, surrounded by a bunch of oblivious bystanders.

"Can I give it a try here, like we did last time?" I grinned.

"No way," Hannah said, pulling the toy out of my hands. "There'll be no trial runs for this or any future tests. You'll just have to wait until we get to the church."

"And where will *you* be sitting while this is all going down?" I said.

"Right next to you, of course. I'll want a front-row seat to watch all the action."

On Sunday morning, Hannah picked me up and drove me the two miles to our local church. The entire time I squirmed in my seat trying to imagine what it would be like having a vibrator buzzing inside me in the quiet chapel. When we got to the church parking lot, she pulled into a sheltered space then plucked the blue vibrator out of her purse and handed it to me, resting her arm on the seat cushion expectantly.

"*What?*" I said. "You don't trust me to put it in privately?"

"Not really," she smirked. "For all I know, you might pull on some adult diapers under your skirt to hide any unintended releases. Here," she said, handing me a plastic vial. "I brought some lube to make it go in easier."

"I don't need any," I said, pulling the vibrator out of her hands and placing it under my skirt. "I'm already plenty worked up thinking about this scenario."

"I hope you're wearing panties under that skirt," Hannah said, watching me shift my weight as I placed the device against my vulva. "We wouldn't want it popping out at an inopportune moment."

"I'll just have to leave that up to your imagination," I sneered, lifting my skirt halfway up my thigh. "Unless you need to inspect the goods to make sure I'm not cheating."

"I trust you," Hannah smiled, opening her car door. "Something tells me you're looking forward to this just as much as I am."

As we approached the entrance to the church, I noticed a familiar figure standing at the top of the steps greeting the incoming parishioners, and he made eye contact with me when Hannah and I approached the landing.

"Jade!" Father Fife said, holding out his hands to me. "I haven't seen you in such a long time. It's so good to have you join us again."

"I'm sorry, Father," I said, placing my sweaty hand between his. "I've been a little distracted lately..."

"Life has a habit of getting in the way of the important things," he said. "We're just glad to have you whenever you can find time." He turned to Hannah, raising his eyebrows in curiosity. "And who's this lovely lady you've brought with you to attend our service today?"

"This is Hannah," I said, motioning toward my friend. "I thought I'd bring her along for moral support."

"Happy to have you, Hannah," Father Fife said, clasping Hannah's hands warmly. "The Lord knows we all need moral support wherever we can find it."

Hannah nodded politely, then the two of us walked through the entrance doors where I dipped my hand into the bowl of holy water and crossed my chest before continuing on toward the front of the chapel.

"*Jesus*," Hannah whispered, peering around the imposing shrine. "Is it just me, or did that feel a little creepy? All that talk about *having* us and that prolonged hand-holding. Hasn't he been paying any attention to the me-too movement?"

"I'm not sure any of that applies to men of the *cloth*," I chuckled. "But you better be careful about using the Lord's name like that around here. If anybody overhears you, you're liable to be burned at the stake."

The two of us stepped lively down the main aisle and finding a free spot in the front row, we took our seats flanked by two elderly couples. It was hard to imagine how Hannah would be able to use the remote-control device sandwiched so closely between other parishioners, and I crossed my legs, thankful for the brief respite. When everyone had filed into the chapel and the bell signaled the start of the service, a hush fell over the chamber and we all stood up as Father Fife walked onto the pulpit in his flowing robes.

"In the name of the Father, and of the Son, and of the Holy Spirit," he intoned solemnly.

"Amen," the congregation murmured in unison.

"The Lord be with you," he said.

"And with your spirit," the couples beside me retorted.

What the hell have I gotten myself into? I thought, feeling the flexible vibrator pressing against the inside of my closed legs. I didn't consider myself a terribly religious person, but being in this holy place surrounded by all the familiar rituals brought back all the old memories from my parents about the consequences of sinful behavior. *Surely getting secretly stimulated by a sex toy in the house of God will send me straight to hell.*

This was the point in the church service where everybody was supposed to take a moment to make a penitential act. While I listened to the other parishioners around me making their supplications, my knees began shaking as I made my own silent prayer for forgiveness.

"May Almighty God have mercy on us all," the priest said. "Forgive us our sins, and bring us to everlasting life."

"Amen," I joined in the congregation's response.

"Let us pray," Father Fife said, bowing his head.

As we closed our eyes and he began his opening prayer, Hannah nudged me with her knee and my mind raced with images of the pastor scornfully looking down at us while we played our blasphemous game. I peered up as he flapped his Bible closed, and caught him glancing in my direction.

"Through our Lord Jesus Christ, your Son," he said. "Who lives and reigns with you in the unity of the Holy Spirit, one God forever and ever."

"Amen," I said aloud, hoping he'd see me behaving like a good Catholic girl and turn his attention elsewhere.

He motioned for everyone to sit down and I was glad to get off my shaky feet onto the relative safety of the wooden pew.

"Good morning, ladies and gentlemen," he began his homily. "Today, I would like to talk with you about *morality*. Specifically, about the decaying state of society's morals in today's world. All around us we are surrounded by prurient symbols of modern decadence. First it was in the form of the printed word, then motion pictures, then the ubiquitous internet. It seems everywhere we turn, we are bombarded with profane and sacrilegious images."

I felt my heart pounding in my chest, like he was singling me out personally for my not-so-infrequent porn surfing.

"We seem to have forgotten," he railed, "the Lord's commandment that we shall not covet thy neighbor's wife. This admonition can be taken in its broadest context. Not only have many of you forsaken the sacred institution of marriage, but the egregious and widespread popularity of obscene *pornography* belies our unbridled lust and depravity. God slew Onan for spilling his seed, and so He will strike all others who practice self-abuse."

Hannah nudged her knee against mine, suddenly

reminding me why we were here. I was glad that she hadn't yet had the opportunity to take out her remote-control device, and I prayed that we'd be able to get through most of the service without her rudely interrupting it. I'd already begun to regret agreeing to this little venture, and I hoped that somehow we'd be able to bypass this first phase in her experiment.

"I'd like you to pick up your Bibles," Father Fife said, interrupting my thoughts. "And turn to Mark, Chapter 7, Verse 20."

Hannah and I reached down to pick up the bibles lying on the seat beside each of us, and we flipped to the indicated section.

"Read this passage with me, my friends," Father Fife instructed. "What comes *out* of a person is what defiles him," he enunciated, while the congregation quietly murmured along.

As I began to recite the passage along with him, I saw Hannah reach into her side pocket and place her closed hand between the book binding.

"For from within come evil thoughts," I continued reading as I peered out of the corner of my eye to see what she was up to.

"Sexual immorality, adultery, coveting, wickedness..." we read in unison.

Suddenly, I felt the interior end of the vibrator begin to tremble inside me and I stuttered, trying to finish the passage.

"Deceit...sensuality...envy..." I stammered, trying to catch my breath as I followed along. Hearing my labored recital, Hannah turned her head in my direction, acknowledging my silent suffering. She knew exactly what I was feeling and how difficult it was for me to remain composed as I read the script.

"All these evil things...come from *within*," I gulped as I began to feel the pleasure spread across my pelvic region. "And they defile a person."

"Consider these words carefully," the priest said, surveying my hunched-over posture. "For the Lord does not abide salacious thoughts and behavior. If you want passage into His Kingdom, you must be as pure and righteous as He."

He paused for a moment to let the message sink in, then he motioned with his two hands for us to be seated. I was grateful for the rest, and I froze upright in my chair trying to ignore the movement of the possessed instrument inside me.

"Let us consider for a moment *another* one of God's ten commandments," Father Fife continued. "Thou shall not commit *adultery*. The Lord made Eve from the flesh of Adam, and in so doing signified that forever more man shall be united to his wife as one..."

As Father Fife ramped up the intensity of his gayphobic critique, so did Hannah, furtively adjusting the flywheel on the remote-control device nestled under her palm in her lap. As she slowly increased the speed of the vibrations emanating inside my pussy, I squirmed on the bench, trying to restrain my rising passion.

"By rejecting the sanctity of marriage," Father Fife continued, glancing distractedly in my direction, "you have all *sinned*. In the book of Deuteronomy, we saw that God ordered adulterers be stoned to death. For your indiscriminate behavior, so shall the Lord indiscriminately smite thee."

Jesus, I thought. If that's what awaits a sinner for

cheating on their spouse, I wonder what happens to someone who self-abuses herself while sitting for Sunday Service in a house of God. *Surely I'll burn in hell for this act of sacrilege.*

Just when I thought I was beginning to get control over the delicious sensations stimulating my insides, Father Fife instructed us to stand once again and recite another passage from the Bible.

"Please stand now and read Peter 1:16 with me," he said.

Everyone stood and dutifully flipped to the relevant section of the scriptures. This time it was even harder for me to stand motionless, as my knees fluttered unsteadily from the pleasurable sensations radiating inside me.

"It is written..." I tried to read along. "That you shall be holy, for I am holy."

I saw Hannah's hands moving once again inside her prayer book, and suddenly I felt the *other* end of the U-shaped vibrator buzzing against my clit.

"And now Galatians 5:16," Father Fife instructed, barely giving me a chance to recover.

I flipped to the new citation and gasped for breath as my legs wobbled beneath me.

"But I say," I panted unsteadily. "Walk by the Spirit, and you will not gratify the desires of the flesh."

"So it is written," Father Fife said, closing his Bible. "Be righteous as the Lord, and you shall join him in Heaven for everlasting days. And now," he said, magnifying my torture. "I would like us to sing together one of my favorite hymns celebrating His blessing, *Amazing Grace.* Please pick up your hymn books and turn to page forty-three."

"Amazing grace, how sweet the sound," the priest began to sing as the entire congregation joined him in harmony.

"That saved a wretch like me," I sang along, trying to

ignore the message that seemed targeted directly at me. As I tried to hold the melody, Hannah cupped the remote-control device in her hand and turned the flywheel to its maximum setting.

"I once was lost, but now am found," I hyperventilated, pressing my legs together as hard as I could to stifle the rising passion that threatened to overtake me.

"Was blind, but now I see," I squealed, singing the last word decidedly off-pitch as Father Fife turned to see my entire body shaking as I belted the famous hymn.

By the time I'd finished the song, I'd somehow managed to keep it together and fight off the cresting passion that had threatened to put me over the edge. When we finally sat back down, Hannah mercifully turned the vibrator off, and I spread my hands over my ruffled skirt to signal that I'd managed to keep myself composed.

When the service was over and we walked up the aisle behind the rest of the assembly to exit the church, I couldn't wait to get out of the building to wash myself off, figuratively and literally. I was glad that we were at the back of the crowd so nobody could see the back of my skirt. I wasn't sure if my leaking pussy had left a stain, but I sure as hell didn't want one of the parishioners pointing it out. When we finally exited the entrance doors, Father Fife turned to the two of us and smiled.

"I noticed you seemed a little more passionate than usual reciting today's passages, Jade" he said to me.

"Yes, Father," I said, shaking his hand unsteadily. "I felt truly embodied by the spirit."

"And *you*, Hannah," he nodded. "Did you enjoy today's service also?"

"Oh yes," she said. "It was the most moving sermon I've attended in a long time."

"I hope you'll both come again," Father Fife said to the two of us.

"I'm sure we *will*, Father," Hannah smiled as we continued down the steps.

Like the second we get back home, I thought to myself, dying to tear off my clothes and squirt all over Hannah's face while she ate out my still-dripping pussy.

READ MORE...

ABOUT THE AUTHOR

If you would like to receive notification of new book(s) in Jade's Erotic Adventures, follow me at http://bookbub.com/authors/victoria-rush.

If you have a moment, please post a brief review on my Amazon book page at viewbook.at/theexchangestudent . Even just a couple of sentences will help other readers find and enjoy this book as much as you hopefully did.

Follow, share, like, and comment at:

www.facebook.com/authorvictoriarush
www.pinterest.com/authorvictoriarush
www.twitter.com/authorvictoriarush
authorvictoriarush@outlook.com

Hope to see you again soon!

www.ingramcontent.com/pod-product-compliance
Lightning Source LLC
Chambersburg PA
CBHW051713180726
48283CB00004B/1322